Dear Parents:

Congratulations! Your child is taking the first steps on an exciting journey. The destination? Independent reading!

STEP INTO READING® will help your child get there. The program offers five steps to reading success. Each step includes fun stories and colorful art or photographs. In addition to original fiction and books with favorite characters, there are Step into Reading Non-Fiction Readers, Phonics Readers and Boxed Sets, Sticker Readers, and Comic Readers—a complete literacy program with something to interest every child.

Learning to Read, Step by Step!

Ready to Read   Preschool–Kindergarten
• big type and easy words • rhyme and rhythm • picture clues
For children who know the alphabet and are eager to begin reading.

Reading with Help   Preschool–Grade 1
• basic vocabulary • short sentences • simple stories
For children who recognize familiar words and sound out new words with help.

Reading on Your Own   Grades 1–3
• engaging characters • easy-to-follow plots • popular topics
For children who are ready to read on their own.

Reading Paragraphs   Grades 2–3
• challenging vocabulary • short paragraphs • exciting stories
For newly independent readers who read simple sentences with confidence.

Ready for Chapters   Grades 2–4
• chapters • longer paragraphs • full-color art
For children who want to take the plunge into chapter books but still like colorful pictures.

STEP INTO READING® is designed to give every child a successful reading experience. The grade levels are only guides; children will progress through the steps a̶t̶ ̶t̶h̶e̶i̶r̶ ̶o̶w̶n̶ ̶s̶p̶e̶e̶d̶, developing confidence in their reading.

Remember, a lifeti̶m̶e̶ ̶o̶f̶ ̶r̶e̶a̶d̶i̶n̶g̶ ̶b̶e̶g̶i̶n̶s̶ ̶w̶i̶t̶h̶ ̶a̶ single step!

D1053972

FIVE
TANK ENGINE TALES

Thomas the Tank Engine & Friends™

CREATED BY BRITT ALLCROFT

Based on The Railway Series by The Reverend W Awdry.
Compilation copyright © 2015 Gullane (Thomas) LLC.
Thomas the Tank Engine & Friends and Thomas & Friends are trademarks of
Gullane (Thomas) Limited.

HIT and the HIT Entertainment logo are trademarks of HIT Entertainment Limited.

Visit us on the Web!
StepIntoReading.com
randomhousekids.com
www.thomasandfriends.com

Educators and librarians, for a variety of teaching tools, visit us at RHTeachersLibrarians.com

ISBN 978-0-385-38496-4

MANUFACTURED IN CHINA
10 9 8 7 6 5 4 3

HIT entertainment

THOMAS & FRIENDS

FIVE
TANK ENGINE TALES

Based on The Railway Series by
The Reverend W Awdry
Illustrated by Richard Courtney

Step 1 and Step 2 Books

Random House 🏠 New York

CONTENTS

AS SEEN ON DVD!

Stuck in the Mud

Based on The Railway Series
by the Reverend W Awdry

Illustrated by Richard Courtney

Click-clack!

Click-clack!

Thomas puffs
down the track.

Thomas finds
an old engine.

Hiro is broken.

Will he be sent to the scrap yard?

No!

Thomas will fix him.

Uh-oh!

Here comes Spencer!

"I'm going to tell!"
says Spencer.

Oh, no!

Hiro needs help!

Thomas puffs off
to get help.

Thomas and Spencer
race down the track.

Splat!

Spencer falls into the mud!

Now Thomas must help
<u>two</u> engines.

He tells Sir Topham Hatt.

Clang! Clang!

Bang! Bang!

Hiro is fixed.

But who will

help Spencer?

Thomas is too small.

Hiro will.

He huffs and puffs.

He pulls Spencer
out of the mud.

"Thank you,"
says Spencer.

Hooray for Hiro!

Click-clack!

Click-clack!

All the friends steam
down the track.

THOMAS & FRIENDS™

DAY OF THE DIESELS

Flynn Saves the Day

Based on The Railway Series
by the Reverend W Awdry

Illustrated by Richard Courtney

Percy rolls
down the track.

Uh-oh!

Percy smells smoke!

Oh, no!
Percy sees a fire!

45

Thomas is in trouble!

Who will save him?

Clickety-clack!

Clickety-clack!

Percy finds Flynn.

Flynn is a fire engine.

Flynn is fast.

Flynn is fearless.

Flynn will save Thomas.

Chuff! Chuff!
Clang! Clang!
The engines
hurry to help.

Smoke swirls.
Flames flash.
The engines
work together.

54

Percy clears
the track.
Thomas is free!

Flynn fights the fire.

Whoosh goes the water!

The flames flicker.

They fizz.

They fade.

The fire is out.

Thomas is safe.

"Good job, Flynn!"

"Thank you, Percy!"

TROUBLE IN THE TUNNEL

Based on The Railway Series
by the Reverend W Awdry

Illustrated by Richard Courtney

Peep! Peep!

Thomas was going
to the Mainland.
Cranky lifted him
onto a raft.
"Goodbye!" called Thomas.

The boat sailed to sea.

Thomas bobbed
behind on the raft.

Soon night came.

Thomas could not see.

But he could hear.

Crack! Crash!

The chain snapped.

"Help!" cried Thomas.

The boat
chugged away.
Thomas was all alone.
Thomas was scared!

The next morning,
the raft floated
to a far-off island.

How would Thomas find
his way back to Sodor?

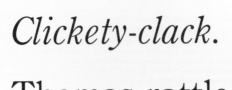

Clickety-clack.

Thomas rattled around a bend.

Then—*screech!*

He stopped.

Three strange engines
were in front of him!

"I'm Bash," said one.

"I'm Dash,"
said another.

"I'm Ferdinand,"
peeped the last.

The new engines said
they could help Thomas.
But they were silly.
They made jokes.
They teased Thomas.

He huffed away.

He puffed up hills.

He chuffed past rocks.

He raced along the track.

Thomas was lost.

Now he *needed* help!

Thomas found Bash,
Dash, and Ferdinand.
"I need help,"
said Thomas.
"Will you tell me
how to get home?"

The engines took Thomas
to an old tunnel.
"This leads to Sodor,"
they said.

They puffed inside.

The tunnel was dark.

The tracks were twisty.

Smash! Crash!

Rocks tumbled down.
Thomas and the engines
were stuck!

The engines had a plan.
They told Thomas to
puff as hard as he could.
Puff-puff-puff!
Thomas' puffs rose
high into the sky.

Back on Sodor,
Percy wondered
where Thomas was.

Then he saw three puffs!

"Thomas!" cried Percy.

He whooshed away

to get help.

Clickety-clack.

Clickety-clack.

Thomas heard something
in the tunnel.

"We'll save you!"
peeped Percy.
The engines from Sodor
bashed through the rocks.

Thomas was rescued.

Hooray!

THOMAS
& FRIENDS™

BLUE
MOUNTAIN
MYSTERY

Secret of
the Green Engine

Based on The Railway Series
by The Reverend W Awdry

Illustrated by Richard Courtney

Thomas is going
to Blue Mountain Quarry.

Thomas is happy
to help
at the quarry.

Thomas sees
a green engine.
He does not know
the engine.

Thomas follows
the green engine.

It speeds up.

Thomas speeds up, too.

The bridge is broken.

"Look out!"

peeps Thomas.

Screech!

The green engine stops.

"Who are you?"
asks Thomas.
The green engine
is scared.

"My name is Luke,"
he says.
"I have to hide,
or I will be sent away."

Luke tells Thomas
that a long time ago,
he did a bad thing.

He bumped

a yellow engine,

and it fell into the water.

It was a mistake.

"If the yellow engine
is found," Luke says,
"I will not have to
hide anymore."

"I will find
the yellow engine,"
peeps Thomas.

Chug! Chug! Chug!
Thomas races
along the track.

Thomas searches

Tidmouth Sheds.

Percy does not know
the yellow engine.

Thomas chugs

to the docks.

Gordon does not know
the yellow engine.

Thomas visits
the Steamworks.
Victor knows
all the engines
on the Island of Sodor.

Thomas asks Victor about the yellow engine.

"I was the yellow engine,"
says Victor.

Thomas is surprised.

Victor fell into the water.

Cranky saved him.

A fresh coat of paint
made Victor
clean and new.

Thomas has found
the yellow engine!
He races
to tell Luke.

Luke does not
have to hide.
Now he can
work at the quarry.

And now Thomas and
Victor have a new
friend!

AS SEEN ON DVD!
KING OF THE RAILWAY
THE MOVIE

TREASURE ON THE TRACKS

Based on The Railway Series
by The Reverend W Awdry

Illustrated by Richard Courtney

Bring the soap!

Bring the water!

Scrub, rinse, and repeat.

The engines are
squeaky-clean.
They are
ready to greet
a special guest.

The guest is
the Earl of Sodor.

The earl
tells the engines
about his special plan.

He will rebuild
the old castle.
Thomas will help.

Thomas and Percy
chuff up the hill.
The castle is old.

The walls are broken.
There is rubble
all around.

Thomas takes
a closer look.

It is not rubble.

It is treasure!

He finds armor.

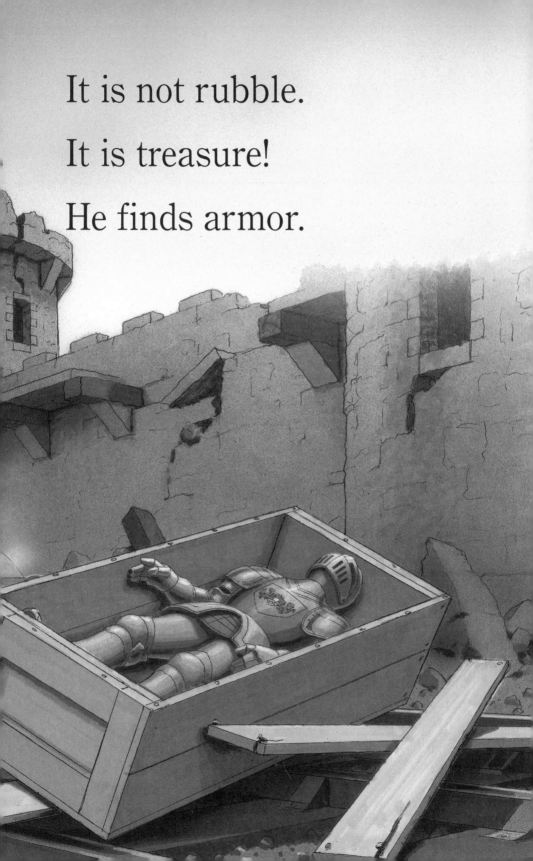

The earl has
a special engine.
His name is Stephen.

Stephen is old.

He needs repairs, too.

Thomas brings Stephen to the Steamworks.

Clink! Clang! Clunk!

Victor makes Stephen

as good as new.

Stephen wants to help.

What job can he do?

Some engines
make repairs.
Stephen cannot reach.

Some engines
carry cargo.
Stephen cannot
carry much.

Some engines
move stone.
The stone is too heavy
for Stephen.

Stephen is sad.

He chuffs off alone.

Uh-oh!

Trucks are coming.

Look out, Stephen!

CRASH!

Thomas searches
for Stephen.

Stephen is safe!
And he found
something special.

It is a king's crown!
It belongs
at the castle.

The earl gives Stephen
his new job.

He has the perfect job.

He helps at the castle!

Hooray for Stephen!